ICHTYOSTEGA

NODOSAUR

SCELIDOSAURUS

ARIZONASAURUS

NYCTOSAURUS

BARYONIX

DRACOREX

CAMARASAURUS

RUGOPS

CHIROSTENOTES

JANE YOLEN

How Do Dinosaurs Say

Happy Chanukah?

Illustrated by

MARK TEAGUE

SCHOLASTIC INC.

All over the world, Jewish people
celebrate Chanukah (or Hanukkah)
in many different ways. We're guessing
no two families celebrate the eight days exactly
the same! So how *do* dinosaurs say happy Chanukah?
With an abundance of love, joy, memory, and gratitude.
—J.Y. & M.T.

To Team Stemple

J. Y.

To the Levi Family

M. T.

Does a dinosaur act up
on Chanukah nights
when Mama comes in
with the holiday lights?

Does he fidget
and fuss through
the candlelight
prayer?

Does he blow out
the candles when
no one is
there?

Does he peek at the presents stashed under Dad's bed?

ICHTYOSTEGA

Does he write

his own name on

each gift card

instead?

And the very next day
does he grab up
the gelt,

squeezing the
candy coins
till they all
melt?

Does he snatch away dreidels

so no one else plays?

Does he do this for each
of the eight festive days?

No . . .

a dinosaur doesn't.

He sings every prayer,

CAMARASAURUS

takes turns with the dreidel,

remembers

to share.

He eats up his latkes,
helps clear away
dishes,

gives Bubbie and Zaida

big Chanukah

wishes.

Each time he's in bed,
for eight nights,
hear him snore.

Happy Chanukah, Happy Chanukah,

you good dinosaur!